DISCARD

To Simon
and
to Julian

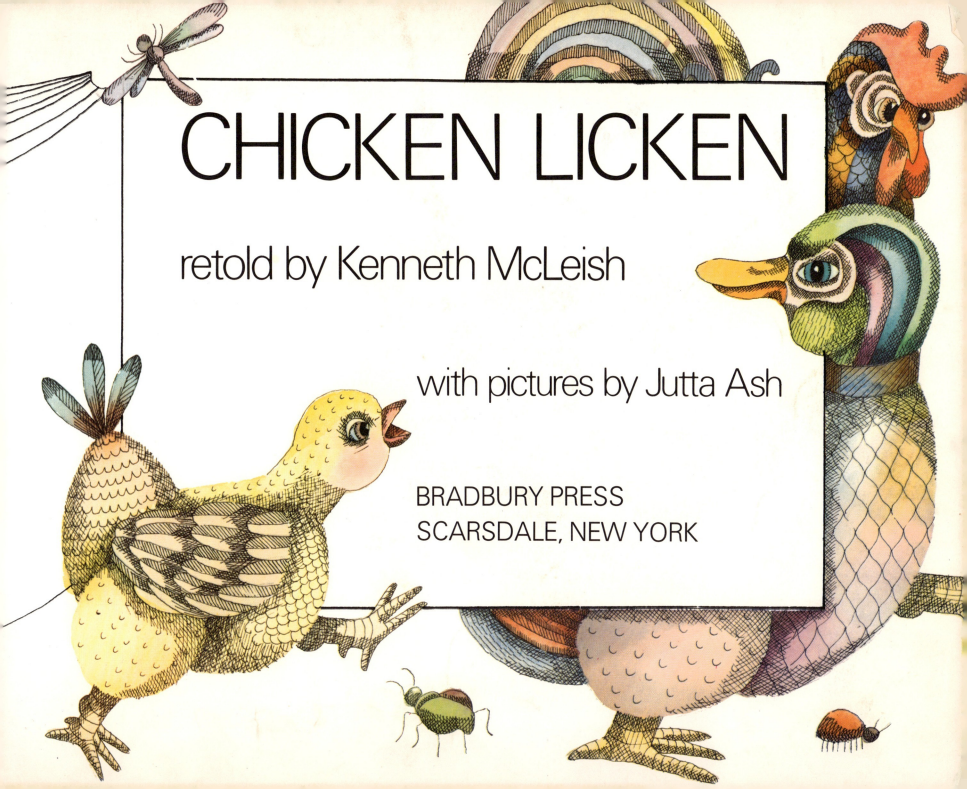

CHICKEN LICKEN

retold by Kenneth McLeish

with pictures by Jutta Ash

BRADBURY PRESS
SCARSDALE, NEW YORK

Text Copyright © 1973 by Kenneth McLeish
Illustrations Copyright © 1973 by Jutta Ash
All rights reserved. No part of this book may be
reproduced in any form or by means, except for the
inclusion of brief quotations in a review, without permission
in writing from the publisher.
Library of Congress Catalog Card Number: 73-81975   ISBN 0-87888-065-8
Printed in the United States of America
First American edition published by Bradbury Press, Inc., 1974
Second printing 1975
The text of this book is set in 18pt. Univers Light with 6pt. leading.
The illustrations are line drawings with color washes, reproduced in full color.

CHICKEN LICKEN

One fine morning, Chicken Licken was walking in the wood . . .

. . . when an acorn fell on his head.
 "Cheep!" he said. "Cheep cheep! The sky has fallen. I must go and tell the king."

He went on walking through the wood. On the way he met Hen Len.

"Chook chook!" said Hen Len. "Where are *you* going this fine morning?"

"Cheep cheep!" said Chicken Licken. "I was walking in the wood, when the sky fell on my head. Now I'm going to tell the king."

"Chook chook!" said Hen Len. "I think I'll come as well."

Chicken Licken and Hen Len walked on through the wood. On the way they met Cock Lock.

"Cockereekoo!" said Cock Lock. "Where are *you* going this fine morning?"

"Chook chook!" said Hen Len. "Chicken Licken was walking in the wood, when the sky fell on his head. Now we're going to tell the king."

"Cockereekoo!" said Cock Lock. "I think I'll come as well."

Chicken Licken, Hen Len and Cock Lock walked on through the wood. On the way they met Duck Luck.

"Waark waark!" said Duck Luck. "Where are *you* going this fine morning?"

"Cockereekoo!" said Cock Lock. "Chicken Licken was walking in the wood, when the sky fell on his head. Now we're going to tell the king."

"Waark waark!" said Duck Luck. "I think I'll come as well."

Chicken Licken, Hen Len, Cock Lock and Duck Luck walked on through the wood. On the way they met Turkey Lurkey.

"Gobbledy gobbledy!" said Turkey Lurkey. "Where are *you* going this fine morning?"

"Waark waark!" said Duck Luck. "Chicken Licken was walking in the wood, when the sky fell on his head. Now we're going to tell the king."

"Gobbledy gobbledy!" said Turkey Lurkey. "I think I'll come as well."

Chicken Licken, Hen Len, Cock Lock, Duck Luck and Turkey Lurkey walked on through the wood. On the way they met Fox Lox.

"Arf arf!" said Fox Lox. "Where are *you* going this fine morning?"

"Gobbledy gobbledy!" said Turkey Lurkey. "Chicken Licken was walking in the wood, when the sky fell on his head. Now we're going to tell the king."

"Arf arf!" said Fox Lox. "And do you know the way to the king's palace?"

"Cheep!" said Chicken Licken.
"Chook!" said Hen Len.
"Cockereekoo!" said Cock Lock.
"Waark!" said Duck Luck.
"Gobbledy!" said Turkey Lurkey.

They all looked at Fox Lox.
  "No," they said. "We don't know the way at all."
  "But I know the way," said Fox Lox. "I'll show you." So Fox Lox took Chicken Licken, Hen Len, Cock Lock, Duck Luck and Turkey Lurkey along the road through the forest.

Do *you* think he showed them the way to the king's palace? Of course he didn't. He took them home to his own house instead.

Mrs Fox Lox and all the baby Fox Loxes were waiting there for dinner.
"Arf arf!" said Fox Lox. "Look what *I've* brought home!"

So Chicken Licken, Hen Len, Cock Lock, Duck Luck and Turkey Lurkey never reached the king's palace.

And the king never knew that the sky had fallen.

But all the Fox Loxes had a *lovely* dinner.